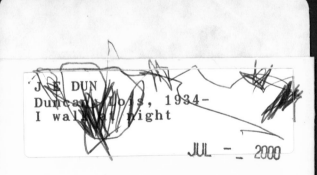

I WALK AT NIGHT

For Ben Johnson,
   with happy wishes
                    —L. D.

For Jordan
                    —S. J. & L. F.

I WALK AT NIGHT

by Lois Duncan

paintings by Steve Johnson and Lou Fancher

VIKING

I walk at night.

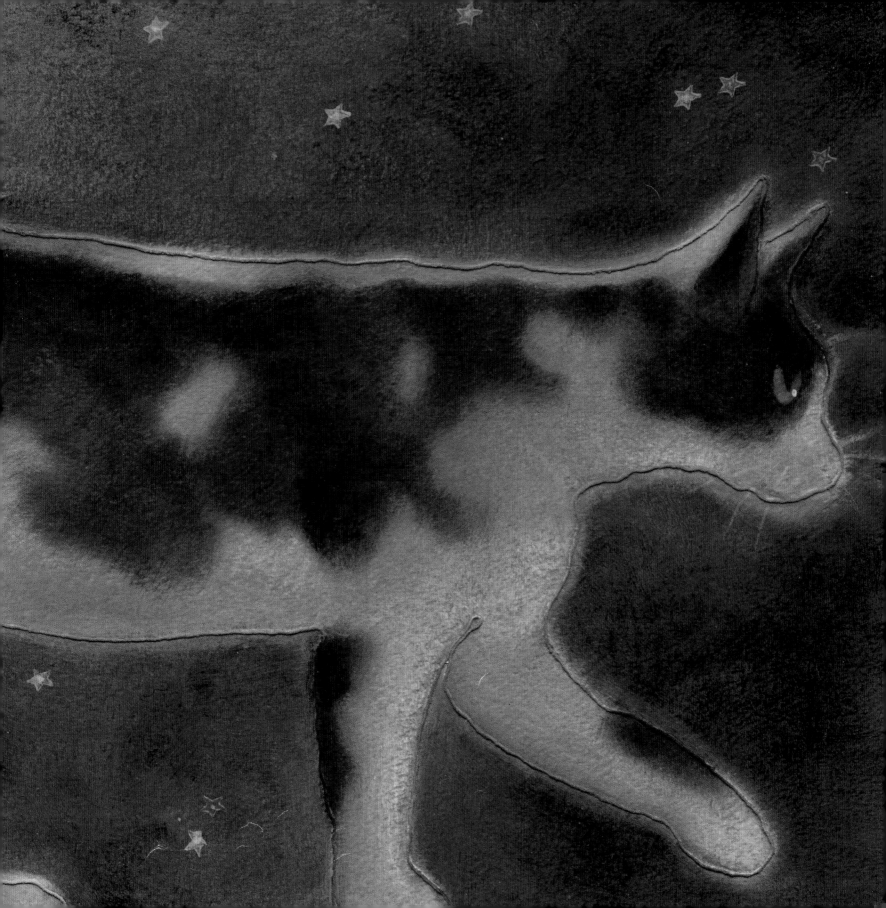

I tread on silken toes.
I wear my furry clothes
Even in clover.

I sit on windowsills.
I watch to see what spills
When things tip over.

I lap from china bowls.
I clean off dishes.

I like the taste of cream,
But while I drink I dream
Of birds and fishes.

In the dark of the night,
I sing as I creep along walls.

In the bright
       morning light,
I mew as I
       saunter down halls.

There once was a time when I
Leapt from the limbs of trees,
Clawing and screaming.

Now in your lap I lie,
Purring a lullaby,
Twitching and dreaming.

Pet me and hold me,
Praise me and scold me,
Snuggle me tight.

For when your eyelids close,
I tread on silken toes,

Drawn by sweet memories
Of caves and jungle trees,

Making my way once more
Out through the kitty door

Into the night.

VIKING
Published by the Penguin Group
Penguin Putnam Books for Young Readers, 345 Hudson Street, New York, New York 10014, U.S.A.

Penguin Books Ltd, Registered Offices: Harmondsworth, Middlesex, England

First published in 2000 by Viking, a division of Penguin Putnam Books for Young Readers.

10   9   8   7   6   5   4   3   2   1

LIBRARY OF CONGRESS CATALOGING-IN-PUBLICATION DATA
Duncan, Lois, date
I walk at night / by Lois Duncan ; illustrated by Steve Johnson & Lou Fancher.
    p.   cm.
Summary: A cat describes the ways in which it enjoys spending the
day and night.
ISBN 0-670-87513-9 (hc.)
[1. Cats Fiction] I. Johnson, Steve, date ill. II. Fancher,
Lou, ill. III. Title.
PZ7.D9117Iam   2000   99-32057   CIP

Printed in Hong Kong
Set in Sanvito

The paintings in this book were created with string and oil paint on paper.
Book design by Lou Fancher